Caesar's Bday Trip

Written and Illustrated by

Michele Charles

CAESAR'S BDAY TRIP

Library of Congress Control Number: 2019902966
ISBN: Softcover 978-1-7960-2132-5
Hardcover 978-1-7960-2133-2
EBook 978-1-7960-2131-8

This is a work of fiction. Names, characters, places and incidents either are the product of the author's imagination or are used fictitiously, and any resemblance to any actual persons, living or dead, events, or locales is entirely coincidental.

Print information available on the last page

Rev. date: 04/01/2019

To order additional copies of this book, contact:
Xlibris
1-888-795-4274
www.Xlibris.com
Orders@Xlibris.com

For Melissa, Who Believes in Dreams,
And still Wishes on Stars.

Everybody has a birthday. Today is Caesar's birthday. Lady gives Caesar a birthday cake and tells him to "Make A Wish".

Caesar and Lady decide to take a trip to find out more about birthday cake, candles, and wishes.

They go into the Klozzitravel and put on their Invisible Goggles.

When they arrive at Candle Kingdom, Colonel Candle is making a speech, "Your ultimate purpose is to grant wishes on birthdays. When you get wished on your wick ignites and you forever shine in Birthday Cake Lake. This is how dreams come true."

Wick sees Caesar and Lady when they
remove their invisible Goggles.

Caesar is dreaming BIG as Lady and
Wick introduce themselves.

"Hello, I'm Wick, Just waiting for someone to make a wish on me so I can forever shine in Birthday Cake Lake to make dreams come true."

"Hi I'm Lady and this is my friend Caesar. It's his birthday, so we're trying to find out more about birthday cake, candles, and wishes."

Caesar and Lady look at Wick in disbelief as a flame grows on his head and he soars into space to join the other candles in Birthday Cake Lake.

Wick smiles and says, "Happy Birthday Caesar! Look for me out your bedroom window. See me shining and know your dreams are coming true!!"

Lady and Caesar don't say much on their ride home in the Klozzitravel wearing their Invisible Goggles.

They are too busy dreaming BIG...

...and wishing on stars.

Sweet Dreams!

CPSIA information can be obtained
at www.ICGtesting.com
Printed in the USA
BVHW021026140419
545471BV00010B/307/P
* 9 7 8 1 7 9 6 0 2 1 3 2 5 *